THIS WALKER BOOK BELONGS TO:

For remembering the best...

First published 2006 by Walker Books Ltd
87 Vauxhall Walk, London SE11 5HJ

This edition published 2007

2 4 6 8 10 9 7 5 3 1

This book has been typeset in Berling

Printed in China

British Library Cataloguing in Publication Data:
a catalogue record for this book is available from the British Library

ISBN 978-1-4063-0377-3

www.walkerbooks.co.uk

Hooray for Harry

Kim Lewis

WALKER BOOKS
AND SUBSIDIARIES
LONDON • BOSTON • SYDNEY • AUCKLAND

Harry the elephant wanted a nap.
When he went to lie down, his bed was bare.
His fluffy old blanket just wasn't there.
"Oh!" said Harry. "My blanket has gone!"

Harry and his friends, Ted and Lulu, started looking for Harry's blanket.

Harry searched the cupboard.

Ted emptied the toy-box.

Lulu looked under the bed.

But the three little friends
couldn’t find Harry’s blanket.
“Where, oh where,
did I put it?” said Harry.

"Did you leave your blanket outside?" asked Lulu.

Harry had a little think. "Oh!" he cried. "I remember! We made a tent in the long, tall grass. We all crawled in."

"We did!" said Ted.

But when Harry, Ted and Lulu ran outside,
the blanket tent in the grass had gone.

“What did we do next?”
wondered Lulu.

Harry had another think.
"We made a sail for my boat!"
said Harry. "I was the captain
and you were the crew.
My blanket blew in the wind."
"I looked for pirates!" said Ted.

But when the three little friends ran to Harry's boat, there wasn't a blanket sail on the mast.

“Hmmm,” said Lulu. “What happened then?”

“We made a swing in the trees!” said Harry.

“We all went swoop!” said Ted.

Harry, Ted and Lulu ran to the trees.

But the trees didn’t have a blanket swing.

“We must have done something else…” said Lulu.

Harry tried thinking a little bit more.
"Oh!" cried Harry. "Now I remember!
We had a picnic in the garden.
We all sat on my blanket."

"I ate up all my picnic," said Ted.
"My blanket got very sticky..." said Harry.
"I know!" said Lulu. "We washed it!"

The three little friends
ran to the bucket.
"But your blanket's not in here," said Ted.
"My lovely blanket," said Harry.
"I thought it would be here. I really did."
"Never mind, Harry," said Lulu.
"You'll remember where it is in a minute."

“Don’t worry, Harry,” said Ted.
“We’ll find your blanket. I know we will.”

So Harry tried thinking, just one more time.

Harry thought of his blanket, so fluffy and soft.
He thought very hard. He thought and thought.

My blanket was a tent,
then a swing and a sail.
Our picnic made it all
sticky. We washed it
and washed it
and then…

What did we do with my drippy wet blanket?

"Oh!" cried Harry. "NOW I REMEMBER!
We hung my blanket to dry!"

Harry ran as fast as he could to the line.

Lulu and Ted ran after Harry.

And there was the blanket, dancing in the wind,
fresh and clean and just waiting for Harry.

"My blanket," cried Harry. "I found you!"

"Hooray for Harry!" cried Lulu and Ted.

"You remembered where it was after all," said Lulu.

"I knew you would," said Ted.

"I'd NEVER forget my blanket," said Harry.

The three little friends cuddled up for a nap.

"I love my blanket," sighed Harry.

WALKER BOOKS BY KIM LEWIS

FLOSS • JUST LIKE FLOSS

EMMA'S LAMB • ONE SUMMER DAY

FRIENDS • MY FRIEND HARRY • THE LAST TRAIN

A QUILT FOR BABY • LITTLE BAA

GOODNIGHT HARRY • HERE WE GO, HARRY

HOORAY FOR HARRY